Amelia Bedelia & FRIENDS

Blast Off

Daisy

me!

Holly

Joy

Rose

Teddy

Clay

Wade

ip

Pat

Candy

Cliff

Dawn

Heather

Penny

Angel

Amelia Bedelia

& FRIENDS

Blast Off

me

by **Herman Parish**

pictures by **Lynne Avril**

Greenwillow Books

An Imprint of HarperCollins Publishers

Special thanks to Rebecca Ann Coles,
PhD Astrophysics, for her invaluable input.

Art was created digitally in Adobe Photoshop.
Amelia Bedelia is a registered trademark of Peppermint Partners, LLC.
Amelia Bedelia & Friends Blast Off. Text copyright © 2021 by Herman S. Parish III. Illustrations copyright
© 2021 by Lynne Avril. All rights reserved. No part of this book may be used or reproduced in any
manner whatsoever without written permission except in the case of brief quotations embodied in critical
articles and reviews. Printed in the United States of America. For information address HarperCollins
Children's Books, a division of HarperCollins Publishers, 195 Broadway, New York, NY 10007.
www.harpercollinschildrens.com

Library of Congress Control Number: 2021942171
ISBN 978-0-06-296193-8 (hardback)—ISBN 978-0-06-296192-1 (paperback)

21 22 23 24 25 PC/LSCH 10 9 8 7 6 5 4 3 2 1

 Greenwillow Books

To Andy and Sarah,
My favorite space cadets

—H. P.

For Ellie and Ben, with love!

—L. A.

Amelia Bedelia

Finally

Joy

Clay

Heather

Cliff

Wade

Dawn

Skip

Angel

Penny

Candy

Contents

Chapter 1

~~shooting~~ A Star Is Born

On Monday morning, every single girl in Mrs. Shauk's classroom found an invitation on her desk. Except for Amelia Bedelia. She didn't need to invite herself.

You are cordially invited to a BACKYARD CAMPOUT SLEEPOVER!!

When: Friday at 6:30 PM
Where: Amelia Bedelia's backyard
B.Y.O.S.B.A.P. (Bring Your Own Sleeping Bag And Pillow)
Pick-up Saturday morning 10:00 AM

Amelia Bedelia and her friends talked about the sleepover all week, until Friday finally rolled around and the sleepover was in full swing.

The back door flew open, and Amelia Bedelia's mother stepped outside holding a tray full of treats. "Is everyone ready for dessert?" she called.

"Yes!" cried Amelia Bedelia and her friends.

"Are we having s'mores?" Daisy asked eagerly.

"We haven't had dessert yet!" said Amelia Bedelia. "How can we have some more?"

s'mores!

"Not some more," said Daisy. "S'mores!"

Amelia Bedelia's mother set down the tray full of marshmallows, chocolate bars, and graham crackers on a log by the campfire.

"You can't have some more s'mores until you have your first one," Amelia Bedelia said. "So let's go find some roasting sticks!"

Amelia Bedelia and her friends scattered, everyone searching the backyard for the perfect stick to toast a marshmallow. It had to be the just the right length. Too long and your marshmallow might fall off into the fire. Too short would put you way too close to the flames.

After getting into a tug-of-war with her dog, Finally, over what both of them thought was the perfect stick, Amelia Bedelia joined her friends around the campfire. She gazed at their faces, glowing in the firelight. She had invited all the girls in her class to the backyard sleepover, and to her delight, everyone was there. Even Angel, who didn't like sleepovers very much. And Penny, who was going to have to wake up super early for her Saturday morning science class, had been determined to come anyway. Candy was the most excited. Amelia Bedelia guessed she hadn't gone to a lot of backyard campout sleepovers in Chicago, where she used to live.

Joy, who liked her marshmallows only lightly toasted, finished her s'more first. With a contented sigh, she leaned against a log and looked up at the sky. "Hey, I see the Big Dipper!" she said, pointing. "That's my favorite constellation."

Holly shook her head. "Don't you remember from science class?" she said. "What Ms. Garcia said was that the Big Dipper is actually an asterisk."

Heather laughed. "No it isn't," she said. "An asterisk is a symbol shaped like a star.

It's used to note something in writing.*
Ms. Garcia was talking about a group of
stars, usually part of a constellation. She
called it an asterism."

Polaris
the
North Star

Ursa Major

"That's right," said
Dawn, nodding.
"It's part of the
constellation called
Ursa Major."

"That means 'great bear' in Latin,"
added Angel. "People back then thought
that it was shaped like a big bear."

Amelia Bedelia squinted at the night
sky. She could definitely make out the
bowl and the handle of the Big Dipper.
But a bear? She just didn't see it. Maybe
a squirrel, if she almost closed her eyes.

Amelia Bedelia's mother poked at the fire with a stick. Red-hot embers drifted into the air, and Amelia Bedelia watched them, transfixed. "The Big Dipper can help you find the North Star," Amelia Bedelia's mother said. "See the two stars on the outside of the Big Dipper's bowl? They point to the North Star. It's the brightest star in the Little Dipper."

That reminded Amelia Bedelia of something. "The North Star is also called Polaris!" she exclaimed. That was the name of her cabin at Camp Echo Woods, where she had gone last summer.

Now Amelia Bedelia's father joined them. "You're right," he said. "And did you know that from Earth, Polaris doesn't

CAMP ECHO WOODS

appear to move? The rest of the sky in the Northern Hemisphere seems to circle around it as the Earth rotates. That's because the Earth's axis points almost directly to Polaris."

He glanced at the fire. "Well, it's either time to add another log or to put it out," he told them. "Which one is it?"

Amelia Bedelia's mother yawned. "I'm certainly sleepy," she said. "Maybe it's time for you ladies to start getting ready for bed. I'll make sure the tents have enough stakes."

"Steaks?" repeated Amelia Bedelia. "It's too late to start grilling, and we've already had dessert." She shrugged and led her friends inside to wash their sticky hands and faces, put on their pajamas, and brush their teeth. By the time they came back outside, the sky had grown even darker and there were more twinkling stars to look at.

"We're heading in, girls," said Amelia Bedelia's mother. "It's time for us to hit the hay."

"I thought you were tired," said Amelia Bedelia.

"I am very tired," said her mother.

"So go straight to sleep

9

now," said Amelia Bedelia. "The hay can wait until tomorrow to be hit."

Her mother gave her a good-night kiss. "Sleep well, pumpkin," she said. "Good night, girls! Don't stay up too late!"

Amelia Bedelia looked at the sky, awash with stars. "Hey, I have an idea," she said to her friends. "Before we get into our tents, let's stretch out on our sleeping bags and look up at the stars."

Everyone liked that plan. They unrolled their sleeping bags, spread them out on the grass, and lay down.

"Where's that North Star again?" asked Holly, once everyone was settled.

Amelia Bedelia turned on her flashlight and shined it into the heavens, the way

10

she had learned at Camp Echo Woods. "Right there," she said, pointing her beam of light at Polaris.

The girls stared intently at the sky. The only sound was the crickets.

"Do you think they can see us shining flashlights at them?" whispered Angel.

Penny raised up on one elbow to look at Angel. "They?" she said. "Who is they?"

"You know," said Angel. "Whoever lives on those stars."

"You know that our sun is a star, right?" Penny said. Angel nodded. "And that all of those stars you see up there are even bigger and hotter than our sun?"

"Oh. Really?" said Angel.

"So that means no one can live on them," Penny explained. "It's impossibly hot."

"Would you get a really bad sunburn?" Angel asked.

"Way worse," said Penny, sitting up completely. "Think of the worst sunburn you've ever had, times a trillion."

Even though that was hotter than hot, that thought sent a shiver through Amelia Bedelia's body. Even her hand holding the flashlight trembled. It wobbled and sent a bright beam of light right into her parents' bedroom. Her father opened the window and leaned out. "Are you guys okay?" he called down to them.

"We're fine," said Amelia Bedelia. "We're doing a little stargazing." She aimed her light at him and he held up his hand, shielding his eyes.

"Be careful!" he called. "Don't shine your flashlights in a Martian's eyes. He might crash his flying

13

saucer. Good night, sleep tight,
don't let the bedbugs bite!"

"Daddy, we're in sleeping bags!" said Amelia Bedelia. "That's impossible!"

It was quiet again and the crickets chirped louder than ever.

"Do you think there's life on other planets, like Mars?" asked Heather. "Or in other galaxies?"

Amelia Bedelia shrugged. "Maybe," she said.

Just then a big bright light streaked across the whole sky, from one side to the other.

"Oooooooooh!" The girls all gasped together.

OooOooooooh!

"What was that?" Rose asked.

"A spaceship?" said Dawn.

"Are aliens invading?" said Angel.

"That was a shooting star!" Amelia Bedelia exclaimed. "The biggest one I've ever seen."

"And now we all get to make a wish!" added Heather.

Amelia Bedelia squeezed her eyes shut. But what should she wish for? She

15

usually wished for a dog, but now she had Finally. She couldn't really think of anything. . . .

Suddenly she had an idea. She decided to wish for a perfect score on her next test. She smiled and made her wish official by opening her eyes again.

"Is everyone done?" she asked. Her friends all nodded. Then they gathered their sleeping bags, and after a little bit of discussion about who would sleep in which tent, they settled in. Amelia Bedelia, Holly, and Heather were in one tent; Dawn, Daisy, Joy, and Penny in another; and Candy, Angel, and Rose in the third.

Amelia Bedelia snuggled into her sleeping bag. She was warm and cozy.

She could feel her eyelids growing heavy.

"Amelia Bedelia?" Heather whispered.

"Yes?" Amelia Bedelia whispered back.

"Someday I'm going to find out if there is life on other planets!" she said.

"That would be out of this world," said Holly sleepily.

Amelia Bedelia nodded. "Yup, it certainly would be," she said. Then she fell asleep.

Chapter 2

You Wished Upon a Star. . .

When Amelia Bedelia walked into the classroom on Monday morning, Candy rushed right over to her.

"Guess what?" Candy said.

As Amelia Bedelia slipped her backpack off her shoulders, she took a wild guess.

18

"Ummmm . . . you lost a tooth?"

Candy gave Amelia Bedelia a funny look. "No. My wish came true!"

"Really?" squealed Heather from across the room. "That's amazing!"

"What did you wish for?" asked Amelia Bedelia.

Candy pointed to the whiteboard.

"You wished that we'd have pizza for lunch?" said Amelia Bedelia, reading the day's announcements.

"No, not that," said Candy.

"*That.*" She pointed to another section of the board, where Mrs. Shauk had written:

Friday morning class trip to FISHER PLANETARIUM *with Mrs. Shauk and Ms. Garcia Don't forget your permission slips!*

"Whoa!" said Candy. "My wish was to go to the planetarium!"

"Wow," said Amelia Bedelia. "That's amazing!"

"My wish came true, too!" said Daisy. "I wished I could see my grandma, and guess what? My parents said we're

20

taking a trip to see her next month!"

"That's so great!" said Amelia Bedelia, smiling from ear to ear. Those wishes had been made in *her* backyard. She felt kind of responsible.

After lunch Amelia Bedelia and her friends headed to gym class.

"Afternoon, everyone," said their teacher, Ms. Chase. "Today we are going to play dodgeball. First we'll split up into two teams, so we'll need two captains."

Cliff and Clay immediately shot their arms up. Ms. Chase shook her head. "You two were team captains last week," she said. "How about Pat and . . ." She looked around. "Joy?"

Joy gasped and turned to Amelia Bedelia, her eyes shining. "That was my wish!" she whispered. "I've never been picked to be team captain before!"

"Amazing," said Amelia Bedelia.

Quickly Joy assembled her team, which included Amelia Bedelia, and led them to victory.

Joy had a huge grin on her face. "That was part of my wish too!" she said.

After gym, it was time for science class. As Amelia Bedelia settled into her seat, she noticed that Ms. Garcia had drawn the solar system on the whiteboard using colored markers. Saturn looked especially pretty with its multicolored rings.

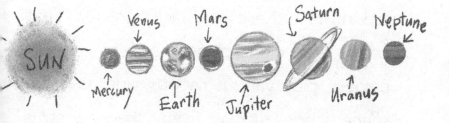

"Let's sum up what we learned about space last week," Ms. Garcia began. "I'll start with an easy one. Wade, you live on . . ."

"Cranberry Lane," he answered.

"A little less specific," said Ms. Garcia. "I was looking for the planet."

"Oh, sure! Planet Earth!" said Wade, sounding slightly embarrassed.

Ms. Garcia continued. "As we discussed last week, our solar

system is made up of one star, which we call the sun, and all the objects that revolve around it and are held in its gravity. That consists of eight planets and five dwarf planets, plus various moons, and assorted space debris left over from when our solar system was formed. And our solar system is just one small part of our galaxy. Does anyone remember what our galaxy is called?" she asked.

"It's on the tip of my tongue," said Chip.

Amelia Bedelia turned around and stared at Chip. His mouth was closed, so she could not see what was on his tongue, the tip or elsewhere.

"I'm pretty sure it has something

to do with chocolate," Chip said.

Ms. Garcia laughed. "That's a good way to remember it," she said. "Can you recall what *kind* of chocolate?"

Heather raised her hand. "The Milky Way?" she said.

"That's right!" said Ms. Garcia. "There are around 100 billion stars in the Milky Way, which is only one of trillions of galaxies. So that will give you an idea of just how many stars there are in space."

"Wow," said Joy. "Just wow."

Angel raised her hand. "So how does a star become a shooting star?

Ms. Garcia shook her head. "Would you believe that a shooting star isn't actually a star? It's a meteor."

"I can't believe it!" said Skip. Then he thought for a minute. "Um, what's a meteor?"

"A meteor is a space rock that enters the Earth's atmosphere," explained Ms. Garcia. "It gets really hot as it travels and starts to burn up, and as it burns, it leaves a glowing trail behind it."

"Do meteors ever reach

the Earth?" Penny wondered.

"Occasionally meteors are so big that they do make it all the way down to Earth before they completely burn up," said Ms. Garcia. "Those are called meteorites. They have a fine specimen at the planetarium. We'll see it this Friday!" She clapped her hands together excitedly. Clearly, she was as thrilled as Amelia Bedelia and her friends about their upcoming field trip.

The bell rang, and Ms. Garcia positioned herself by the door. "Don't forget to bring in your permission slips!" she called as everyone trooped out. "Also, we'll be having a test on our solar system on Monday."

As Amelia Bedelia headed out of the classroom, she crossed the fingers on both hands for good luck. A science test! She hoped that *her* wish would come true next.

Chapter 3

▫ ▫ ▫ Now Here You Are!

At last Friday morning arrived. Amelia Bedelia, her friends, and Ms. Garcia were standing in front of Fisher Planetarium, waiting for Mrs. Shauk, who was inside getting their tickets. Amelia Bedelia craned her neck to look up at the big building.

"We've got an hour before we

head into the planetarium for the show," said Ms. Garcia. "You're in for a treat!"

A treat! This was good news to Amelia Bedelia. Breakfast felt like a long time ago already, and a snack sounded like an excellent idea.

Penny poked her in the back. "Look at my new sneakers!" she said, pointing proudly at her feet.

"Super cool," said Amelia Bedelia, admiring her friend's bright pink high-tops.

Penny nodded. "They're what I wished for!" she said.

"Oh, wow," said Amelia Bedelia. So many of their wishes were coming true! She wondered whose wish would be next.

"We're all set," said Mrs. Shauk, joining them. "Now, I expect everyone to be on their best behavior today. Let's file in, please. One at a time. No pushing!" Slowly the class shuffled past her as they headed inside. "That's right," said Mrs. Shauk. "Keep filing, keep filing."

Cliff was behind Amelia Bedelia in line. He laughed.

"Keep filing," she heard him say under his breath. "That's how the Hawk gets her nails so sharp."

Amelia Bedelia glanced at Mrs. Shauk's pointy, blood-red fingernails and nodded. They sure looked sharp.

"Nails?" scoffed Cliff. "When you're the Hawk, they're called talons!"

"*Shhhhh!* No talking. Keep filing," said Mrs. Shauk.

Amelia Bedelia stepped inside. Her stomach growled, but she didn't see any snacks.

"Excuse me," she said to a security guard. "Where are the treats?"

"There is no food

allowed in the exhibit area," the guard replied.

Amelia Bedelia's stomach growled at the guard, loud enough to make him look around for the noisemaker.

Amelia Bedelia was disappointed, but not for long. The planetarium had gotten a spiffy new update since her last visit, and there was so much to see. Large, colorful models of the planets hung from the soaring ceilings. There was a meteorite to touch and a moon rock to admire—so many cool-looking interactive exhibits that she didn't know what to do first.

meteorite

moon rock

Candy grabbed Amelia Bedelia's hand and pulled her over to a display about

comets. "Did you know that Halley's Comet appears every seventy-five years?" she said. "That is so awesome!"

"Look, Amelia Bedelia!" shouted Cliff. He was standing on a metal plate, a digital screen hanging over his head. "I'd weigh one hundred and thirty-one pounds on Jupiter!" He stepped off the scale. "Here, you try it!"

Amelia Bedelia stepped on the scale and pressed a different button. "And I'd weigh twenty-one pounds

What Would You Weigh on MERCURY? 21 lbs

on Mercury!" she announced.

"Somebody get Amelia Bedelia an ice-cream sundae!" joked Mrs. Shauk, who was passing by.

Amelia Bedelia looked around to make sure the security guard had not over-heard. "There is no food allowed in the exhibit area, Mrs. Shauk," she said.

"Good point," Mrs. Shauk replied.

A bunch of Amelia Bedelia's friends were clustered around a display across the room. Amelia Bedelia headed over to check it out. "What are you all looking at?" she asked.

Teddy turned around. "Black holes!" he said. "They're really amazing. They're areas in space where the gravity is so

strong that even light can't
get out of them."

a black hole
in space

"There are four kinds
of black holes," Dawn said.
"Stellar, intermediate, supermassive, and
miniature."

"The one in the Milky Way is
a supermassive black hole," said
Wade. "That's the largest kind
there is!"

Jupiter

X 168!!

"Yeah, it's as wide
as 168 Jupiters in
a row!" added Dawn.

"Really?" said Skip, who had just
joined them. "That's hard to swallow."

"Sounds more like impossible," said
Amelia Bedelia, making a face. "Give me

an ice-cream sundae any day."

Amelia Bedelia strolled from exhibit to exhibit, each one more interesting than the last. She stopped at an exhibit about the Earth's moon. She learned that it is the fifth-largest moon in the solar system. She discovered that the moon does not make its own light but is illuminated by the sun. And that for a long time, people thought that the moon didn't have an atmosphere, but now it is known to have a very thin one called an exosphere.

She had just finished reading about lunar eclipses when she spotted her class lining up at the theater doors. It was almost time for the show to begin.

When the doors opened, Ms. Garcia led Amelia Bedelia and her friends across a row of seats, stopping at the end. "Take a seat," she said.

Amelia Bedelia studied the chair. "I think it's bolted down," she said.

Ms. Garcia shrugged. "It probably is," she said. "Can you sit down?"

Amelia Bedelia nodded. "I sure can," she said.

Ms. Garcia tried again. "Please sit down," she said.

Amelia Bedelia sat. She was happy to discover that the seat was soft and super comfortable, with a neck rest so she could lean back and look up at the ceiling. She couldn't wait for the show to begin.

Chapter 4

Planets on Parade

A young man in a bright blue shirt covered with planets appeared on stage. "Hello, everyone! My name is Todd. Welcome to Fisher Planetarium! We are so glad you joined us today, and I'd like to give a special shout-out to the students of Oak Tree Elementary!"

"Oak Tree in the house!" shouted Clay.

"*Shhhhh!*" hissed Mrs. Shauk.

Amelia Bedelia laughed. *Shhhhh* Oak Tree in the *planetarium* was more like it.

"Now sit back and enjoy the show," said Todd. "Afterward we will have an appearance by a very special guest."

The ceiling lights began to dim, plunging them all into the pitch-blackness of outer space. Amelia Bedelia couldn't even see her hands! Gradually, stars began to appear on the ceiling above them.

"Hey, this looks just like Amelia Bedelia's backyard!" called out someone from the complete darkness. Amelia Bedelia smiled. That sounded like Dawn.

Shhhhh!

"*Shhhhh!*" Mrs. Shauk hissed.

A deep voice began to speak in hushed tones. "Today we are going to take you on an exciting journey through our solar system, which formed 4.5 billion years ago."

The stars above them began to spin. Heather, who was sitting on Amelia Bedelia's right, squeezed her hand tightly. Amelia Bedelia squeezed back.

Then the sky above them grew brighter as the voice continued: "Our first planet, Mercury, is almost 35 million miles away from the sun. It is the smallest planet, a bit bigger than Earth's moon. Even though it is

Mercury
no moons

the closest to the sun, Mercury may still have ice in its craters. Mercury does not have a moon.

"Neither does Venus, our next stop. It is called Earth's twin, as they are almost the same size. Venus is actually the hottest planet in our solar system, because its thick atmosphere traps the sun's heat. Temperatures on Venus can reach 880 degrees Fahrenheit! It is also the brightest planet that we can observe from Earth."

Venus
no moons

Brightest planet? wondered Amelia Bedelia. How could they know that? Did they give Venus an IQ test?

"Venus is one of two planets that spin backward,

so the sun rises in the west and sets in the east there.

"Next, we see a planet you'll recognize right away—our own planet Earth! It appears blue from space, as seventy percent of it is covered in water. It is the only planet that has liquid water on its surface. It's also the only planet in our solar system that can sustain life, as far as we know."

Earth
1 moon

Next, a large red orb began to come into focus.

"Welcome to Mars. We call it the red planet, as its surface is covered in a thin layer of rust. Mars has two moons, as well as the biggest volcano of all the planets. It's called Olympus Mons,

Mars
2 moons

and it is three times taller than Mount Everest."

"What do volcanoes do when you tell them a joke?" whispered Clay. "They *erupt* with laughter!"

hhh! Mrs. Shauk hissed three times in a row. *"Shhhhhh! Shhhhhh! Shhhhhh!" Shhhhhh!*

hhh! Amelia Bedelia gasped as giant Jupiter loomed into view. The narrator continued. "And here we see our largest planet, Jupiter. It is so big that all the other planets could fit inside it. Jupiter has seventy-nine moons. See that large red spot on its surface? That's actually a storm that is hundreds of years old, with a diameter bigger than Earth!"

"It would be tough to be a

Jupiter
79 moons

weather forecaster on Jupiter," whispered Cliff. "Your only storm to track has lasted hundreds of years."

"A day on Jupiter is less than ten hours long," said the all-knowing voice.

"At least you'd have a short workday," said Clay.

Amelia Bedelia shook her head. How would you get any sleep on Jupiter? She was glad she lived on Earth, where they had twenty-four-hour days.

Everyone *ooh*ed and *aah*ed as the beautiful rings of Saturn came into view. "Saturn is the second-largest planet and a gas giant. It has distinctive rings, which are made of chunks of ice

Saturn

and rock. Saturn's largest moon, Titan, has its own atmosphere," the narrator continued. "Next up is Uranus, the ice giant. It is called the sideways planet because it spins on its side. It also spins in the opposite direction from Earth, like Venus. It is the coldest planet. Like Saturn, it has rings, but they are not as easy to see, since they are thin and dark.

Uranus

"Our eighth and final planet, Neptune, is another ice giant. It has fourteen moons and is the windiest planet, with gusts over eleven hundred miles per hour.

Neptune
14 moons

"And now we're heading home. Hold on to your seats!"

Amelia Bedelia grabbed her armrests. The planets began to flash by as they headed back in the direction of the sun.

"I'm getting seasick," Wade said.

"That's impossible," responded Teddy. "We're millions of miles away from water."

"Then I'm getting spacesick," Wade answered.

"This concludes our tour of the solar system," said the narrator. "Thank you for being a part of our incredible space mission. Welcome back to Earth!"

The lights slowly came up, and everyone blinked as their eyes adjusted. The young man in the bright blue shirt reappeared. "And now we have a treat for you," he said. "Let's give a warm Fisher Planetarium welcome to our very special guest today— retired astronaut Lisa Donovan!"

"Oh, wow, a real astronaut!" said Heather as Lisa Donovan strode out in her spacesuit to applause and cheers. She had curly red hair and carried her helmet underneath her arm.

"Thank you all," she said. "It is an honor to be here. As a young child, I was obsessed with space. My very first word was 'star.' I spent every weekend at my local planetarium.

When I got older, I decided to become an astrophysicist. That means I studied physics, math, and cosmology."

Amelia Bedelia's hand shot up. "My mom's cousin studied cosmology at Mr. Pierre's School of Beauty!" she said.

Lisa grinned. "Actually, cosmology is the study of how the universe began," she explained. "Though I certainly do enjoy manicures!" She held up her hands, displaying her dark blue polished fingernails. Every nail had a little planet Earth on it.

"After working in research for several years, I applied

for the space program. The day I got the call was the happiest day of my life!" She laughed. "Well, until I went into space, that is. I went to the International Space Station three times, and I've done six space walks."

"How does it feel to be weightless?" Skip asked.

"Pretty weird!" said Lisa. "There's an expression that astronauts use—puffy head, bird legs. That about sums it up. Because you are weightless, the fluid from the bottom part of your body moves up. Your head feels very stuffy and your legs get very weak and wobbly. But soon you get used to it, and it is an incredible feeling."

"Did you take anything personal with you into outer space?" asked Wade.

"You are allowed to take a few lightweight objects with you," said Lisa. "I took my harmonica and my stuffed crocodile, Neon. When he floated, we knew that we had reached zero gravity."

"What was the most amazing thing you saw from outer space?" Dawn asked.

Lisa smiled. "I'd have to say that it was looking down and seeing Earth. There are no boundaries or borders between countries. Nothing that separates one place or people from another. It's all one big beautiful blue Earth."

Heather raised her hand. "How many times have you been to Saturn?" she asked.

"Aha! A girl after my own heart," said Lisa.

Amelia Bedelia grew alarmed. "You can keep your heart, Ms. Donovan," she said. "Heather's heart works fine."

Lisa laughed. "I mean that Saturn is my favorite planet too," she explained. "When I was little, I imagined skating on its icy rings. But the truth is that no one has ever been there, or any of the other planets. Their atmospheres just won't allow it. But four robotic spacecraft have been sent to observe Saturn, and the last

Cassini

one, the *Cassini*, was there for thirteen years. And who knows? With advances in technology, maybe one of you might reach Saturn someday. Or at least one of its moons!"

A little boy in the front row spoke up. "I was wondering how astronauts go to the bath—"

Todd interrupted. "And that's all the time we have, folks! If you'll line up right here, you can shake Lisa's hand and get a photo taken with her!"

"The closest I've ever come to a real astronaut before today was when my grandpa brought me freeze-dried ice cream back from the Smithsonian,"

Rose said to Amelia Bedelia when they were on the bus headed back to school.

Holly leaned across the aisle. "Hey! That reminds me," she said. "My aunt is picking me up and taking me to Lickety Splits for a hot-fudge sundae today."

"Yum," said Amelia Bedelia.

"That was my wish, you know," Holly told her.

"Wow," said Amelia Bedelia. "That was one powerful shooting star!"

"You mean meteor," said Holly.

"Hey!" called Clay. "Why didn't the astronaut like the restaurant on the moon?"

Mrs. Shauk was in a very good mood. "Please tell us," she said.

"The food was good, but it had no atmosphere!" he yelled.

Amelia Bedelia shook her head. "Yes, it does," she said. "It has an exosphere!"

Chapter 5

Remember Mnemonics!

On Sunday evening, Amelia Bedelia sat at her desk studying her notes on the solar system. She let out a loud, long sigh.

Her mother poked her head into her room. "Anything wrong, cupcake?" she asked.

"Just studying for my science test," said Amelia

Bedelia, pushing back her chair. "I can remember the names of the planets, but not in the right order."

"Oh, that's easy," said her mother. "My Very Educated Mother Just Served Us Nachos!"

"Huh? Did Grandma really bring over nachos?" Amelia Bedelia said, jumping up. "With chili and lime and sea salt and . . . ?"

Amelia Bedelia's mother laughed. "Sorry to let you down," she said. "That phrase is a mnemonic device."

"A nim what?" asked Amelia Bedelia.

"*Ni-mon-ic* device," repeated her

58

mother. "It's a way to help you recall something. You can remember notes on a musical scale by reciting Every Good Boy Does Fine. Or the order of the colors in the rainbow by saying Roy G. Biv."

"It works!" said Amelia Bedelia. "Red, orange, yellow, green, blue, indigo, and violet!"

My = Mercury
Very = Venus
Educated = Earth
Mother = Mars
Just = Jupiter
Served = Saturn
Us = Uranus
Nachos = Neptune

Her mother nodded. "Exactly!"

Amelia Bedelia frowned. "There's just one problem," she said. "I'm also supposed to memorize the dwarf planets. Do you have a nim . . . nim . . ." She gave up. "A special way to remember all of them too?"

"What are the dwarf planets called?" her mother asked.

Amelia Bedelia read her notes. "Ceres, Pluto, Haumea, Makemake, and Eris." She showed her mother the diagram she had drawn in class.

"We can do this . . . but it's going to be a mouthful!" said her mother. She sat down on Amelia Bedelia's bed, patting a spot next to her.

Amelia Bedelia hopped up next to her mother. "Oh, goody," she said. "I could use a snack."

Amelia Bedelia's friends were waiting for her when she arrived at school on Monday morning.

"Two more wishes came true!" Rose squealed.

"Whose?" asked Amelia Bedelia.

"Mine!" said Dawn. "I wished we'd

61

have breakfast for dinner. And last night we did!"

"Lucky you," said Amelia Bedelia, feeling a tiny bit jealous. Her family had eaten meatloaf the night before, her third-least-favorite dinner.

meatloaf

"Mine came true too," said Angel. "I wished for a new cage for my pet snake, Squeezer, and my dad brought one home last night!"

Amelia Bedelia reached into her backpack and pulled out her notebook. She turned to a clean page and quickly made a list of all the friends who had been at her sleepover, placing checkmarks next to the names of those whose wishes had come true.

She stared at her name. She hoped
she hadn't wasted her wish. Sure, she
had studied really hard for her test, but a
little magic wouldn't hurt. She sighed and
headed to science class. She'd find out
soon enough.

"Class, I've graded all your tests," Ms. Garcia announced a couple of days later. "Some of you didn't do as well as I'd hoped, and I'd like to make sure you understand the material." She walked up and down the aisles, placing the tests facedown on student's desks, as she always did.

Skip lifted his paper and groaned. "Oh no, I bombed the test!" he said.

"It looks okay to me," said Amelia Bedelia. Inside, she felt very nervous. Her wish could be the first meteor wish not to come true! She folded her hands on her desk and waited,

sitting very still.

Ms. Garcia paused next to Amelia Bedelia. "So how did you prepare for this exam, Amelia Bedelia?" she asked.

"My mom helped me with some moronic advice," Amelia Bedelia said.

Ms. Garcia looked surprised. "She did?"

"Yup," said Amelia Bedelia. "We made up a saying to remember the order of all the planets and dwarf planets."

"Oh, a mnemonic device!" asked Ms. Garcia. "Great idea. What is it?"

Amelia Bedelia cleared her throat. "My Very Energetic Monster Chef Just

Served Us Nachos, Pancakes, Hamburgers, Marshmallows, and Eggrolls," she recited. She smiled. "It's all my favorite foods!"

"Served by a monster chef who is full of beans!" said Ms. Garcia.

"No, definitely not beans," said Amelia Bedelia. "None of the planets start with B."

Ms. Garcia nodded solemnly. "That's true. Well, I can understand why you did so well," she said. "And I'd love for you to teach that trick to the rest of the class." She placed the test on Amelia Bedelia's desk and headed to Clay's desk.

Amelia Bedelia held her breath and flipped the test over. And there, in Ms. Garcia's crisp writing, it said:

With a huge grin, Amelia Bedelia took out her notebook and placed a big fat check next to her name. Now there were only two friends left whose wishes hadn't come true yet: Rose and Heather.

Chapter 6

To Florida for Fun

"I'll be out most of next week," Heather told Mrs. Shauk on Friday. "My aunt's wish came true. She got a ring."

"From Saturn?" said Amelia Bedelia.

Heather gave her a funny look. "No, silly, from her boyfriend.

Well, now he's her fiancé. They're getting married next week in Florida."

"Oh, how fun!" said Mrs. Shauk. "I love weddings. And warm weather too."

"We're also going to visit Cape Canaveral while we're there," Heather said.

Mrs. Shauk explained to the class that a "cape" was a point of land jutting into the ocean. Cape Canaveral was a cape in Florida where, over the years, thousands of missiles and rockets had been launched into outer space, including the mission that first landed astronauts on the moon.

"I hope you'll get a chance to visit

Kennedy Space Center," she said. "Take lots of pictures. You can give us a full report when you return."

A full report! That sounded like a lot of work to Amelia Bedelia, but Heather seemed happy to oblige.

At recess, Amelia Bedelia and her friends were sitting around the tree stump table, comparing their favorite things to do in Florida, when Rose joined them. Her eyes were shining, and she had a big smile on her face.

"What's going on?" asked Dawn. "You look like you're about to burst!"

"Should I go get Nurse Payne?" asked Amelia Bedelia, standing up.

"I'm fine," said Rose. "I'm just excited!

My wish came true yesterday!"

"Ooh!" said Candy. "What did you wish for?"

"A pet!" said Rose. "And guess what? My neighbor found a stray kitten in her backyard, and my parents are letting me keep him!"

"That's amazing!" said Amelia Bedelia. She had to remember to check off Rose's name as soon as she got back to the classroom.

"I named him Meteor," said Rose. "He's so cute! He's fluffy and gray and has big blue eyes." She sighed. "I just love him."

"Sounds adorable," said Dawn. "It seems like the stars are lining up for us."

Amelia Bedelia laughed, imagining the stars lining up the way she and her friends did at school every day.

"Talking about stars lining up . . . ," said Heather. "Have you guys ever heard about astrology?"

"Isn't that what we're learning about now?" asked Daisy.

"That's astronomy," explained Heather. "Although they are both about objects in the sky." She placed a book on the tree stump. It had the moon, the sun, and several stars on the cover. "Astrology is the belief that the position of the stars and the planets can affect people's life on Earth." She patted the book. "My mom is totally into horoscopes. You know, your birth sign? There are twelve of them. It's cool because each sign has its own constellation. I'm Sagittarius, the archer. I'm adventurous!"

Sagittarius
the archer

"You definitely are," said Holly.

"And I'm a Leo, the lion. I'm bold and brave."

"My sign is Cancer, the crab," offered Angel. "I'm supposed to be sensitive, loyal, and creative." She smiled. "And I guess I kind of am."

Leo
the lion

"What am I?" asked Rose. "My birthday is March first."

Heather consulted the book. "That means you are a Pisces. The fish."

Cancer
the crab

Pisces the fish

Rose wrinkled her nose. "Ewwww," she said. "Do I have to be? I don't really like fish."

"You could try changing your birthday," said Cliff.

Heather looked up from her astrology book. "It says here that Pisces people are artistic and musical."

Rose giggled. "I *do* enjoy playing the kazoo," she said.

"Do you really believe that stuff?" asked Candy.

"No. It's not science. But sometimes I read my horoscope in the newspaper," admitted Penny. "One time mine said I was going to come into some money, and later that day I found a five-dollar

bill on the sidewalk!"

Heather nodded. "And once mine said
I was going to go on a trip and that very
day my mother took me to . . ."

"Hawaii?" guessed Amelia Bedelia.

". . . the mall," finished Heather.

Candy did not look convinced. "I
don't know," she said. "Seems like you're
grasping at straws," she said.

"Oh no, we can't do that. They don't

let us use straws at school anymore," explained Amelia Bedelia. "They're bad for the environment." Amelia Bedelia looked at Heather. "Does your horoscope say anything about a wish coming true?" she asked. "You're the only one left."

Heather closed the book with a bang. She sighed. "I don't think my wish is ever going to come true," she said. "It's a little bit . . . out of this world." She stood up and tucked her book under her arm. "See you guys later," she said, and headed across the playground.

"I wonder what her wish was," said Candy. She turned to Holly. "Do you know?"

Holly frowned. "She hasn't told me. But I think I figured it out," she said.

"What is it?" Joy asked.

"I'm pretty sure that she wished she could go to Saturn," Holly said. "Think about it. She said her wish is out of this world. Plus, you heard what she asked the astronaut."

Joy shrugged. "It already came true, kind of. We flew past Saturn at the planetarium."

"No, I think Heather wants to land on Saturn for real," said Holly.

"I'm not going to hold my breath waiting for that wish to come true," said Joy.

"Why would you do that?" asked Amelia Bedelia.

"I'm not going to," said Joy. "Because it's never going to come true."

"Okay, good," said Amelia Bedelia. "Because once my cousin held his breath for so long, he almost passed out. I would not recommend it."

Chapter 7

Not Wishy-Washy

That evening, Amelia Bedelia and her parents had breakfast for dinner to celebrate her perfect grade on her science test.

"You are never going to believe it," said Amelia Bedelia. She chomped on a piece of bacon.

"Okay, I won't," said her

father, reaching for the last
blueberry pancake.

For the first time in her life, Amelia
Bedelia was speechless. She really did not
know what to say. And since her father
was never going to believe whatever she
said, why should she say anything? They
sat in silence for a minute until her mother
spoke up.

"Ignore him, Amelia Bedelia," said her
mother. "Try me."

Amelia Bedelia turned toward her

mother and tried again. "You're never going to believe it," she said. "Remember when we had the backyard campout sleepover?"

"Yes, we remember," said her mother.

"Well, after you went in to punch the hay, we saw a shooting star—I mean, a meteor—and everyone made a wish. And now every one of those wishes has come true! All except for Heather's."

"Wow," said her mother. "I believe you."

"So do I," said her father "What did everyone wish for?"

Amelia Bedelia popped her last bit of bacon into her mouth and began listing the wishes on her fingers. "Candy wished to go to the planetarium. Daisy wished to visit her grandma. Penny wished for new sneakers. And Dawn wished for breakfast for dinner."

"Aha, smart girl," said her mother, spearing a piece of pancake.

Amelia Bedelia continued. "Rose wished for a pet. Holly wished to go out for ice cream after school. Joy wished to be team captain. Angel wished for a new cage for her snake, and I wished for a hundred on my next test. And they all came true! Isn't that amazing?"

Amelia Bedelia's father put down his fork. "There is a word for that," he said.

"Amazing!" said Amelia Bedelia. "Or awesome? How about incredible?" She had run out of words.

"We call those coincidences," he explained gently. "Except for your wish. You studied hard. So hard that you got a perfect score. You *made* your wish come true."

Amelia Bedelia thought for a second, then shook her head. "No, I'm pretty sure it was that meteor that made the difference. It had something to do with it."

"What was Heather's wish?" asked her mother.

"To go to Saturn," Amelia Bedelia answered.

"The planet?" Both her parents said it at the exact same time.

"Yup," said Amelia Bedelia.

Her father shrugged. "Heather's wish hasn't come true because it is impossible," he said.

Her mother nodded. "Maybe Heather could make a new wish," she said. "One that has a better chance of coming true."

"Oh no . . . you have that look in your

eye, Amelia Bedelia," said her father. "I
know what that means. You're going to
try to grant Heather's wish, aren't you?"

Amelia Bedelia smiled. "If I was, you
would never believe it."

Chapter 8

Interplanetary Sleepover

On Monday morning after everyone had settled in their seats, Mrs. Shauk began to walk around the room, collecting homework. When she got to Cliff, there was nothing on his desk.

"Where is your

homework, Cliff?" she asked.

Cliff looked down. "My dog ate it," he said sadly.

Mrs. Shauk shook her head and moved on to the next desk. It was also empty.

"And where is *your* homework, Clay?" she asked. "Don't tell me that your dog ate yours too."

"I won't," Clay said. "Because I don't have a dog. But I do have a cat. And—crazy story—he picked up my homework and dropped it into a black hole. And I'm not strong enough to pull it out."

Mrs. Shauk looked like she might laugh. "Fair enough, boys," she said. "You can stay in during recess to complete your missing assignments."

"But Mrs. Shauk, I—" Clay started to say, but Mrs. Shauk cut him off with a glance.

"Those two don't have a leg to stand on," said Skip to Amelia Bedelia.

"I'm pretty sure they have two each," she said. "So that's four."

"What I mean is—"

"Attention, please!" said Mrs. Shauk, clapping her hands. "We are beginning a new unit. We're going to focus on . . ."

Amelia Bedelia felt nervous. Mrs. Shauk hated to be interrupted, but Amelia

Bedelia raised her hand anyway, waving it back and forth to get her teacher's attention.

"Can this wait?" said Mrs. Shauk, slightly annoyed.

"Not if you are starting a new unit," said Amelia Bedelia. "I have an idea for a class project. It's very educational."

Mrs. Shauk perched on the edge of her desk. "I'm all ears," she said.

"You only have two, Mrs. Shauk, just like everyone here," said Amelia Bedelia.

"Two what?" asked Mrs. Shauk.

"Ears," answered Amelia Bedelia.

"True," said Mrs. Shauk impatiently. "So far, so good. Now let's hear your idea."

Amelia Bedelia quickly explained about the slumber party, spotting the meteor, all their wishes, and how everyone's wish had come true except for Heather's.

"She wished that she could visit Saturn," said Amelia Bedelia. "My parents say that's impossible. But what if we could make it come true? Kind of. Sort of? If we made this room look like Saturn?"

"How?" asked Joy.

That one word was all Amelia Bedelia needed to hear. She blasted off like a rocket on a mission, fueled by ideas from herself and her friends. "While she's in Florida, we could decorate our classroom so it looks like a spaceship and have a countdown and launch," she said. "And we could make the hallways and the gym look like Saturn! We could study all about the planet to make it seem like Heather is really there. . . ."

Penny began taking notes. "We don't want any ideas to fall through the cracks," she said.

"We'll even fix the cracks," added Amelia Bedelia. She knew she had done the right thing when Mrs. Shauk smiled. "What a terrific idea!" she said. "Of course we'll have to include Ms. Garcia. The science part is wonderful, but we could also incorporate math with all the calculations, and art with the costumes and decorations. And we can all write a poem about our travels, so that's language arts!"

"Yay!" cheered most of the class. (A couple of kids weren't thrilled about the poem part.)

Mrs. Shauk held up her index

finger. "But my hands are tied until I get permission from our principal's assistant, Mrs. Roman."

Amelia Bedelia stared at Mrs. Shauk's arms. "Did someone use invisible rope?" she asked.

"Trust me, they are tied," said Mrs. Shauk. "Getting permission will be the key, especially if I'm going to ask to have the very first school sleepover!"

This time the entire class cheered.

Later that afternoon, Amelia Bedelia and her friends were in science class when there was a knock on the door. Mrs. Shauk, wearing a huge smile on her face, poked her head in.

"Amelia Bedelia had an idea for a class project," she told Ms. Garcia. "I went to Mrs. Roman to ask her about it, and she's on board!"

"She went on a cruise?" asked Amelia Bedelia. "She could have come with us to Saturn!"

"She's not on vacation," said Mrs. Shauk. "She's just—"

"Tell me more about this project!" Ms. Garcia interrupted.

Ms. Garcia listened intently as Mrs. Shauk explained Amelia Bedelia's idea. But then Ms. Garcia sighed. "I hate to open up a can of worms . . . ," she said slowly.

"Gross! Then don't!" said Amelia Bedelia.

Ms. Garcia continued. "But as your science teacher, I do need to point out that it is quite impossible to visit Saturn. Any spacecraft that attempted to land would be crushed because of the pressure and temperature. Plus, Saturn doesn't even have a surface to land on."

"It doesn't?" asked Candy.

"No, it is a gas giant," she explained.

"Gas!" said Rose. "PU!"

"Not that kind of gas," said Ms. Garcia. "Instead of having a solid surface like Earth, Saturn is made up of gases that are toxic to humans."

"Well, maybe we could land on the rings!" suggested Penny.

"That would be difficult too," said Ms. Garcia. "Saturn's rings are made up of pieces of ice and rock. Some are as small as a grain of sand. Others are as big as a house!" She shook her head. "Plus the electrical currents, the terrible winds, the intense pressure and cold—it's impossible!"

"But it is possible to pretend we are there," said Amelia Bedelia.

"True," Ms. Garcia said. "Saturn *is* my favorite planet—after Earth, of course. Did you know that it is sometimes called the jewel of the solar system? It's just so beautiful, with its wonderful rings." She threw up her hands. "Okay, you've convinced me. This really would be a great way for us to go into depth about our second-largest planet."

"Is it a lot larger than Earth?" asked Holly.

"My, yes," said Ms. Garcia. "More than seven hundred Earths could fit inside Saturn."

You are here 🌍 × 700 = 🪐

"Whoa," said Pat. "That's big."

"How long would it take us to get there?" asked Angel.

"Well, since it's about nine hundred million miles away from Earth, it could take us about eight years," answered Ms. Garcia.

"Eight years! We'd be teenagers by the time we got there!" said Joy.

"You know," said Penny, "some people think that if you travel at the speed of light you wouldn't get any older."

Mrs. Shauk raised her hand. "Sign me up," she said.

"Maybe it's time to introduce you to the theory of relativity," said Ms. Garcia.

"What's that?" asked Wade.

"Just the most famous set of equations in the world," said Ms. Garcia, writing on the whiteboard.

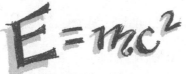

$$E = mc^2$$

"And this is the most famous part of it.

Can anyone read this equation out loud?"

"E equals m c two," read Amelia Bedelia.

"It's E equals mc *squared*," said Ms. Garcia.

"Squared?" said Amelia Bedelia. "But Cs are curved."

"That tiny number two means you multiply that number by itself," said Penny.

"But C is a letter, not a number," said Amelia Bedelia.

"C stands for the speed of light," explained Ms. Garcia. "Light travels 186,000 miles *per second* in space."

Wade let out a low whistle. "That's faster

than I go downhill on my bike," he said.

"A lot faster," said Cliff. "No offense, Wade!"

"Light can travel fast because it is made up of energy and doesn't have any mass to slow it down," said Ms. Garcia. "But even so, the stars are so far away that by the time their light reaches us, the light is thousands of years old. Those stars may not even exist anymore."

Amelia Bedelia felt overwhelmed by all this new information. She began to wonder about everything . . . like, *How can you see something when it is so far away and traveling so fast that it might not exist anymore?* She wished that life was simpler, like it had been a week before.

"So, you see," Ms. Garcia concluded, "it's all relative."

Amelia Bedelia nodded. "That's true in my family. Everything depends on the relative," she said. "My aunts give much better presents than my uncles. Like, for Christmas my aunt Mary gave me a detective kit, while my uncle Dave gave me a box of socks. Itchy ones."

Chapter 9

To Saturn for Science

"My name is I-C-U and I cannot wait to go to Saturn," said Cliff in a clipped robot voice. "How about you, I-M-E-Z-2-C?" He was dressed from head to toe in boxes covered with aluminum foil.

So was Clay. "Affirmative," he said in the same robotic voice. "Saturn is going to be a blast!"

"I see what you did there," replied Cliff.

It was Thursday afternoon, and everyone was excited and a little tired too. It had been a busy week. They had built everything they needed to transform Mrs. Shauk's classroom into a spacecraft. There was a flight deck at the front of the room. It looked very high tech, constructed from a huge box that Mrs. Shauk's new dishwasher had been delivered in. They had made the

spacecraft's front window —a pull-down screen that Amelia Bedelia and her friends had decorated with a big mural studded with stars.

Strands of colorful flashing lights were strung around the room, leading to a control panel the students constructed out of another big piece of cardboard. The control panel was covered with plastic caps—the controls—they had collected from the recycling bin. The spacecraft's hatch was the classroom door. To create their space helmets, they had slathered newspaper strips in a gloopy flour-and-water mix and smoothed them over inflated balloons.

When the newspaper dried, they popped the balloons, leaving the hardened paper behind. And they made oxygen tanks out of empty cereal boxes and water bottles that they painted and decorated.

"We have helmets and oxygen tanks," Mrs. Shauk had said. "But we still need space suits. Does anyone have any ideas?"

Pat raised his hand. "My uncle is a house painter and he always wears these cool white suits to protect his clothes. Maybe he could help us."

"Great idea, Pat. Maybe he'll let us borrow some," said Mrs. Shauk. "Why don't I give him a ring?"

"Aren't you already married, Mrs.

Shauk?" asked Amelia Bedelia.

"Indeed I am," said Mrs. Shauk. "To Mr. Shauk. He once met Neil Armstrong. Do you know who that is?"

"The first man on the moon!" yelled Amelia Bedelia and her friends.

Everyone had worked hard painting, decorating, creating, calculating, and researching to make their space launch as perfect as it could be. They had even borrowed high-powered fans from Pete's Diner and fog machines from the local DJ. Amelia Bedelia and her friends knew Saturn inside and out, from its gaseous surface to its solid rocky core. And now they were ready.

"I can't wait until Heather

comes back tomorrow!" said Daisy. "She is going to be blown away!"

"We can turn the fans down," said Amelia Bedelia.

"We should probably turn them up," said Holly. "The wind on Saturn can blow—"

"More than eleven hundred miles an hour!" the class shouted.

"This was a super-fun project, Amelia Bedelia," said Rose. "Heather is going to be over the moon!"

"I think you mean *moons*," said Amelia Bedelia. "Because we all know that Saturn has—"

"One hundred and fifty moons and

moonlets!" everyone said in unison.

Mrs. Shauk put a hand on Ms. Garcia's arm. "Our work here is done," she said.

"Is she here yet?" Candy asked impatiently.

"Not yet," said Amelia Bedelia. The whole class had arrived early on Friday morning to be there before Heather arrived. Their sleeping bags were piled in a corner of the classroom. But Heather was nowhere to be seen.

"Are you sure she's coming back today?" Rose asked worriedly.

"Her parents know the whole plan," Mrs. Shauk said. "She's coming."

The door opened.

"SUR—" Amelia Bedelia and her friends started to shout.

"Sorry, kids," said Ms. Garcia, looking sheepish as she slipped into the room. "It's just me."

Finally, right as the late bell rang, Heather walked into the classroom.

"SURPRISE!" everyone shouted.

Heather gasped.

"Welcome back," said Mrs. Shauk.

"And welcome to our spacecraft, the *Hawk*," said Ms. Garcia.

Mrs. Shauk looked quite pleased. "Great name," she said. "Thank you."

"We voted on it," said Amelia Bedelia.

Heather looked around, confused. "What's going on?"

"Were your ears burning while you were in Florida?" Mrs. Shauk asked.

"Oh, I hate that," said Amelia Bedelia. "Did you get a sunburn?"

"No," said Heather. "My mom is constantly slathering on the sunblock!"

"I guess she missed your ears," said Amelia Bedelia. She nodded. "It happens."

"Well, Amelia Bedelia told us about your wish," continued Mrs. Shauk.

Heather looked puzzled. "But I didn't tell anyone my wi—"

"We . . . well, actually, *I* figured out what your wish was," said Holly. "Not to toot my own horn or anything."

"That's a great idea," said Amelia Bedelia. "We need a launch party song!"

"A what?" said Holly.

"A song," said Amelia Bedelia. "You can play it on your horn."

"On my what?" said Holly, looking puzzled. She turned back to Heather. "So we decided to make your dream come true!"

"Well, as true as we could without

any of us melting or being crushed by Saturn's oppressive atmosphere," Ms. Garcia interjected hastily.

Heather still looked confused.

"We're going to Saturn," said Amelia Bedelia. "It's going to be an overnight mission."

"Your parents will be dropping off your toothbrush and sleeping bag later," said Mrs. Shauk.

"Oh . . . wow," said Heather. She shrugged off her backpack, sat in her seat, and looked around. She took in the flight deck, the lights, the spacesuits hanging in the coat closet, and the helmets lined up on the windowsill. "You did this all for me?" she said. "But I . . ." Then she smiled. "Oh, that's so thoughtful. I can't wait! I can't believe the whole class is having a school sleepover."

"Everyone but me," said  Teddy sadly. "My dad forgot to sign the permission slip."

"But you have to come with us to Saturn," said Heather. "You are mission critical!"

"Goodness, one visit to Cape Canaveral and you already sound like an astronaut," said Mrs. Shauk.

"That's A-OK with me," said Heather.

It was tough to get any schoolwork done that day. Everyone was so excited. Even though they knew it was pretend, it still felt like they were setting off on an awesome adventure.

When the last bell rang at the end of the day, Amelia Bedelia and her friends sat in their seats and listened to the other students walking down the hallway as they headed home for the weekend.

There was a knock at the door. Mrs. Roman stuck her head into the classroom. "Just wanted to wish you all a safe journey to Saturn!" she said. She gave them a crisp salute and left.

After a long late-afternoon recess where the class drew the entire solar system on the playground in chalk, ate more boxes of pizzas than Amelia Bedelia had ever seen before, and played countless games of seven-up, Marco Polo, and duck, duck, goose, it was finally time for to take off on their mission.

"Wait!" said Pat. "No dessert?"

Just then Mrs. Shauk's cell phone rang. "I'll be right there," she said.

She returned with Pete, who was carrying a big cardboard box from his diner, filled with . . .

"Moon pies!" cried Amelia Bedelia. She loved Pete's chocolate-covered marshmallow sandwich cookies.

"When Mrs. Shauk told me you were heading to Saturn, I couldn't let you take off without the appropriate dessert!" he said.

"Manners, manners . . . ," Mrs. Shauk prompted them.

"Thank you, Pete," the class chorused between bites.

After all the moon pies had been devoured, everyone put on their spacesuits and helmets and sat in their assigned seats. Heather, Amelia Bedelia, and Teddy—whose parents had dropped off his permission slip—took their places on the flight deck and began pushing buttons and spinning dials. The sounds of Mission Control filled the air.

"Booster!"

"Go!"

"Procedures!"

"Go!"

"We are go

for launch," said Heather. "T minus sixty seconds."

A roaring sound filled the room. Amelia Bedelia knew it was a recording that the teachers were playing, but her heart began to beat faster anyway. She looked around at her classmates, who all looked very serious too. She held her breath as they waited to take off.

"T minus fifteen . . . fourteen . . . thirteen . . . twelve . . . eleven . . . ten . . ."

"Ready for ignition," said Angel.

Heather continued counting down: "Nine . . . eight . . . seven . . . six . . . five . . ."

"Starting main engines," said Wade.

He reached over to press a button on the control panel.

Heather resumed her countdown. "Four . . . three . . . two . . . one . . . zero. Booster ignition. We have liftoff!"

Everyone cheered as a roaring sound filled the room. The floor almost felt as though it was shaking.

"We have cleared the Earth's atmosphere," Ms. Garcia announced shortly after. "Let's get out of our spacesuits and ready for bed! We'll be landing on Saturn in about eight hours."

"Not eight years?" said Penny.

"We realized your parents would probably miss

you if you were gone
that long, so we added
this." Everyone clustered
around the control board to see
what she was pointing at. It was a big red
button about the size of a peanut butter
jar lid (because it was a peanut butter
lid) labeled HYPERSPEED in Ms. Garcia's
neat handwriting. "Send us on our way,
Amelia Bedelia," said Ms. Garcia.

Amelia Bedelia pressed the button,
and then she and her friends got into their
sleeping bags. But they were way too
excited to fall asleep.

"Hey, what kind of books do planets
like to read?" Clay asked. "Comet
books!" He launched into his next

joke immediately, "Why couldn't the astronaut focus? He kept spacing out!"

He moved on. "When do you know—"

"That's it, Clay," said Mrs. Shauk firmly. "We're Nep-tuning you out."

"Good night, everyone," said Ms. Garcia. "Time to Sa-turn in!"

"Wake up! We're almost there!" said Heather, eight hours later.

Amelia Bedelia woke up with a start.

She sleepily threw on her spacesuit and helmet and took her place with her fellow astronauts.

"Getting closer . . . ," announced Heather. "Brace yourself . . ."

There was a great roar and suddenly—silence.

Ms. Garcia smiled at the class. "The *Hawk* has landed!"

Chapter 10

A Very Happy Landing

Even though Amelia Bedelia knew she was in her school and not actually about to step out onto the unfamiliar terrain of an unexplored planet, she was surprised at how rapidly her heart was beating. After

everyone had strapped on their oxygen tanks, they lined up by the classroom door. Her friends looked very serious. Even I-C-U and I-M-E-Z-2-C were quiet and not cracking jokes for a change.

"Heather, why don't you do the honors?" said Ms. Garcia, pointing to the control panel by the spacecraft's hatch. "After all, you are the reason we are here today!"

Heather stepped forward and pressed several buttons on the space pad. Then she opened the door.

Amelia Bedelia and her friends stepped into the hallway.

"Ohhhhhh, wow," Holly said.

"It's so windy!" said Rose.

"And foggy," added Angel.

"It's like we're really there!" exclaimed Amelia Bedelia.

"Welcome to Saturn," said Ms. Garcia. "Though the planet has a solid rocky core, it is truly a gas giant. Its surface is a mix of hydrogen and helium, with clouds of ammonia ice that give it its yellow appearance. So please keep your helmets and your oxygen tanks on!"

"After we explore Saturn's gaseous surface, we will conduct experiments on density. Did you know that Saturn is the lightest planet?" said Mrs. Shauk. "As a matter of fact, if you could find a swimming pool that was big enough, you could float Saturn in it."

"Saturn is about nine and a half times wider than Earth," said Joy.

"That's one humongous swimming pool!" said Amelia Bedelia.

"Underneath these gaseous clouds is molecular hydrogen, followed by liquid metallic hydrogen, and finally a rocky core," explained Ms. Garcia.

They walked through a set of doors and past the main office. They pushed through another set of doors and entered another windy hallway, where lights were flashing and there was the sound of rumbling thunder. "Saturn has many storms," said Ms. Garcia. "It has been said that—"

"Has anyone seen Clay?" Mrs. Shauk interrupted.

"That name does not compute," said I-M-E-Z-2-C.

Mrs. Shauk sighed. "Has anyone seen I-C-U?"

"He said he needed to go back to the classroom . . . I mean, the spacecraft," said Chip.

"I'll go find him," Amelia Bedelia volunteered.

She headed down the hallway and pushed

open the doors. She walked past the main office and through the second set of doors. But she was immediately engulfed in a fog as thick as pea soup, which was Amelia Bedelia's second-least-favorite soup.

"Clay?" she called out.

Clay's voice sounded faraway and frightened. "I can't see anything and I can't get this box off my head! I keep bumping into the walls!"

"I'll find you!" called Amelia Bedelia. She walked forward, her arms extended. She stopped. "I have an idea. Let's play Marco Polo. That way we can find each other. Marco!" she called.

"Polo!" answered Clay.

Amelia Bedelia turned toward his voice. "Marco!" she called.

"Polo!" he answered.

Soon she felt a cardboard box.

"Oof! That's me," said Clay. "I think the fog machine is broken!"

"Hold my hand!" commanded Amelia Bedelia. They shuffled forward until her feet hit something. It was the fog machine. She dropped Clay's hand and reached down and located the cord. She followed it until she reached the outlet. She unplugged it carefully.

Amelia Bedelia heard the door swing open. "Oh my goodness!" said Mrs. Shauk's voice. "The fog machine has gone wild! Are you two okay?"

128

"Affirmative!" said I-C-U. "But I think I may need to recharge my batteries!"

"A robot joke!" said Mrs. Shauk. "Sounds like you're just fine."

As the air began to clear, the rest of the class found them. Ms. Garcia opened the windows. "Good thing fog machines run on plain old sugar alcohol and distilled water, not poisonous gases," she said.

"Hey, what are all those people doing on the playground?" asked Teddy.

Everyone peered outside.

"They are certainly trespassing!" said Ms. Garcia. "I'm going to give them a piece of my mind!"

"She can't really do

that, can she?" Amelia Bedelia asked Candy.

Candy shrugged. "If she's mad enough, she sure can," she said.

"There's a lot of them," said Penny. She took another look. "Are they wearing . . . costumes?"

Mrs. Shauk put a hand to her forehead. "Of course! It completely slipped my mind. Mrs. Roman told me she had rented out the playground for some sort of convention." She looked outside.

"Wait a minute," she said. "Is that a Conundran fossilite?" She turned to the students. "Come on, follow me!" she said.

They all stepped outside, and before their unbelieving eyes, Mrs. Shauk clasped her hands together. She raised them in the air, shaking them twice over each shoulder, first her right and then her left. "May the sun always shine on your grublug!" she shouted.

Amelia Bedelia and her friends turned and stared at their playground. There were aliens of all shapes, colors, patterns, and sizes milling about. And every single

one of them stopped what they were doing and did the very same thing back to Mrs. Shauk, answering, "And may your plinkus be plentiful!"

Mrs. Shauk looked at her students. "Have none of you ever watched *Interplanetary Voyagers*? It's only the best sci-fi show in the history of television!"

"Greetings, earthlings!" said a purple-and-pink polka-dotted creature. "Come join our convention!"

A woman with reptile-like skin and six arms stepped up on the tree stump table to address the crowd. "Welcome to the *Interplanetary Voyager* convention," she said. "As everyone knows, I.V., as we like to call it, was the longest-running space show in television history. It is an honor to gather with you all to pay homage to a program that brought so many of us such great joy. And we'd like to extend a special welcome to the earthlings of Oak Tree Elementary for greeting us in costume! How thoughtful, and such a wonderful surprise! We offer you a hearty Folgardian thank you."

The crowd stamped its feet. "Ark ark!" they barked.

There were pins to collect, aliens to meet, and posters to get signed. Amelia Bedelia's arms were soon filled with *Interplanetary Voyager* paraphernalia. She ran into Heather in line at the Cosmic Cantina.

"I'm sorry your Saturn trip got cut short," Amelia Bedelia told her.

But Heather's eyes were shining. "I can't believe it," she said. "My wish came true!"

"I know," said Amelia Bedelia. "You went to Saturn!"

Heather bit her lip. "Actually, that wasn't my wish at all. I didn't want anyone to feel bad, so I just . . . Wow, you guys did so much!"

"You didn't want to go to Saturn?" Amelia Bedelia was puzzled. "So what was your wish then?"

"It was to meet an alien!" Heather said with a laugh. "And do you want to know the funniest part of all?"

"What?" said Amelia Bedelia.

"I should have seen this coming. When I checked my horoscope for this weekend, it said, 'Be sure to clean up for unexpected guests!'"

Chapter 11

Less Moon, More Stars

"Some more s'mores?" asked Amelia Bedelia's mother.

"Yes, please," said Amelia Bedelia, reaching for another marshmallow. It was Saturday evening, and she, her parents, and Finally were having dessert around the campfire under the light of the full moon.

"So what's your big surprise?" Amelia

Bedelia asked after she polished off her second s'more.

"Are you running out of patience?" teased her father.

"I don't think so," said Amelia Bedelia. "I think I still have a good amount."

Amelia Bedelia's mother spread a beach blanket out on the grass. It reminded Amelia Bedelia of summers past when, after a long day at the shore, her parents would each grab an end of their beach blanket and swing her back and forth in the air before packing up to return home.

Now they all settled down on the blanket, Amelia Bedelia between her parents and Finally curled at their feet. Her father checked his watch for the millionth time.

"Are you expecting a UFO, Daddy?" said Amelia Bedelia. "Are little green men going to kidnap you and transport the earthling back to their galaxy?"

Her father tried to change the subject. "So did Heather enjoy the trip to Saturn?" he asked.

"She really did," said Amelia Bedelia. "But it turns out that wasn't her wish, after

all." She explained the story to her parents.

"Oh my goodness," said her mother.

"I used to love *Interplanetary Voyagers*!" exclaimed her father. "Did Heather tell the class the truth?"

"She decided that since the day was so much fun and everyone was so happy, there was no reason to ruin it for anyone," Amelia Bedelia said.

"Well, that was very thoughtful," said her mother.

Her father checked his watch one more time.

"Why do you keep checking your watch?" asked Amelia Bedelia.

"Well, they predicted a heavy shower tonight," he said.

Amelia Bedelia and her mother looked at each other, then at him.

"But it's as clear as a bell," said her mother.

"Yeah, not a cloud in the sky," said Amelia Bedelia.

"I hope not," said her father. "I really want to see this shower, this *meteor* shower. It should be the best of the year."

As soon as he finished talking, a shooting star zipped across the heavens.

Amelia Bedelia looked at her father. "I have been told that there is a word for when things happen at the same time."

"True," he said. "The word is 'planning.'"

"I thought it was 'coincidence,'" said Amelia Bedelia's mother.

"Actually," said Amelia Bedelia's father, "I paid ten dollars to have that star shoot across the sky."

Amelia Bedelia laughed. "Good one, Daddy."

"What does it cost for an eclipse?" asked Amelia Bedelia's mother.

"The usual rate is a hundred dollars, but tonight it is free," he said.

Amelia Bedelia's mother began to laugh, then stopped. The bright full moon was beginning to be covered in shadow.

"A lunar eclipse!" Amelia Bedelia said with a gasp. "The moon is passing through the shadow of the Earth, which is getting between the sun and moon! I learned all about it at the planetarium!"

"That's exactly right, cupcake," said her mother. She sighed. "What a perfect evening. I'm on cloud nine."

"Don't be silly, Mommy," said Amelia Bedelia. "You're right here on Earth!"

As the sky grew darker, it

became easier to see the shooting stars.

"There's a meteor a minute," said Amelia Bedelia.

"That's a lot of shooting stars," said her father. "I've heard that each one comes with a wish."

"I already have what I would wish for," said Amelia Bedelia's mother.

"Me too," said Amelia Bedelia's father.

"Me three," said Amelia Bedelia.

No one had to call for a family hug. They all snuggled closer together against the cool darkness, watching the universe in action.

Two Ways to Say It
By Amelia Bedelia

"Out of this world."

"Hit the hay."

"Really great."

"Go to bed."

"Hard to swallow."

"Don't let the bedbugs bite!"

"Difficult to believe."

"A mouthful."

"Have a good night's sleep!"

"Word(s) that are hard to say."

"Full of beans."

"Has lots of energy."

"Stars lining up."

"Everything is coming together."

"She's onboard."

"She agrees."

"Toot my own horn."

"Bragging about myself."

"On Cloud Nine."

"Feeling extremely happy."

145

SATURN CAKE POPS
They are out of this world!

Ingredients

1 box cake mix (any flavor)

1 can frosting

1 package each yellow and orange candy wafers (aka candy melts)

Wax or parchment paper

18–20 lollipop sticks

1 cookie sheet

Box poked with holes, or glasses filled with rice

1 ziplock bag

Directions

1. Bake cake according to directions on the box.

2. Let the cake cool, then crumble it into a bowl.

3. Add 4 teaspoons of frosting and mix thoroughly. If cake is dry, add a bit more frosting.

4. Roll the cake mixture into Ping-Pong–sized balls. (There'll be about 18 of them.)

5. Microwave a few yellow candy wafers in a mug or other container. Heat the candy 20 seconds at a time, so wafers don't burn.

6. Dip lollipop sticks into the melted wafers and then poke them halfway into the cake pops. Put cake pops on a cookie sheet lined with wax or parchment paper.

7. Freeze the cake pops on the cookie sheet for 20 minutes.

8. Melt a bigger handful of yellow wafers in the microwave.

9. Dip cake pops into the melted wafers. Tap stick gently to remove excess coating, then slowly twirl the pops until coating is smooth.

10. Stand cake pops in the box with holes (or in glasses with rice) to harden.

11. Line cookie sheet with fresh wax/parchment paper.

12. Microwave a large handful of orange candy wafers (20 seconds at a time).

13. Pour the orange melted wafers into a ziplock bag. Snip a small corner, to use it as a piping bag.

14. Measure the diameter of a few cake pops, then carefully draw cake pop–sized circles on the cookie sheet with the melted orange candy. (These will be Saturn's rings!)

15. Put the cookie sheet into the freezer until the rings harden.

16. After the rings harden, place them around the middle of the pops. You may have to gently trim to fit or add some melted chocolate so they will stick.

17. Enjoy your Saturn cake pops!

Ask a grown-up to help with the oven and microwave!

Amelia Bedelia + Good Friends = Super Fun Stories to Read and Share

Amelia Bedelia and her friends celebrate their school's birthday.

Amelia Bedelia and her friends discover a stray kitten on the playground!

Amelia Bedelia and her friends take a school trip to the Middle Ages that is as different as knight and day.

Amelia Bedelia and her friends work to save Earth and beautify their town.

Amelia Bedelia and her friends save their ice cream party!

Amelia Bedelia and her friends are out of this world!

Celebrate the holidays with Amelia Bedelia!

Ho! Ho! Ho! Cookies, presents, snow! It's Amelia Bedelia's favorite time of year.

Boo! Candy, costumes, shivery thrills! Halloween is here.

For Amelia Bedelia, spring will always be as fresh as a daisy!

♥ The Amelia Bedelia Chapter Book

With Amelia Bedelia, anything can happen!

Have you read them all?